Little Red Riding Hood

One sunny day, Little Red Riding Hood set
off to visit her grandma with a basket of food.
"Be careful not to stray from the path," said
her mother, "and don't talk to any strangers."
Little Red Riding Hood promised to be careful,
and waved goodbye.

The little girl soon forgot her promise and left
the path to pick some pretty flowers.
Suddenly a wolf jumped out from behind a tree.
"Where are you going little girl?" he asked.
"To my grandma's to give her some food,"
replied Little Red Riding Hood. The wolf grinned
and licked his lips.

The wolf had a plan. He quickly ran to
Grandma's house and knocked on the door.
"Who is it?" called Grandma.
"It's me, Little Red Riding Hood," said the wolf
in a high voice. Grandma opened the door.
The wolf burst in and gobbled her up! He put on
her clothes and got into bed.

It wasn't long before Little Red Riding Hood arrived
at Grandma's house. She knocked on the door.
"Who is it?" called the wolf in a squeaky voice.
"It's me, Little Red Riding Hood," said the girl.
"I've brought you some food."
"Come in, come in," the wolf replied.

Little Red Riding Hood entered the house and put down her basket. She walked over to the bed. "Grandma," she cried, "what big eyes and ears you have!" "All the better to see and hear you with my dear," said the wolf. "Come closer so that I can see what treats you have brought for me."

Little Red Riding Hood moved closer and sat beside the bed.
"Oh Grandma," she cried, "what big teeth you have!"
"All the better to eat you with my dear!" growled the wolf.
The wolf jumped out of bed and gobbled up Little Red Riding
Hood in one big gulp!

The woodcutter was walking past Grandma's house when he heard a growling noise. He opened the door and couldn't believe his eyes. The big fat wolf was asleep, snoring in Grandma's bed! With one chop from his axe, the woodcutter killed the wolf.

Then he cut open the wolf's fat tummy
and out popped Grandma and
Little Red Riding Hood, alive and well.

The woodcutter dragged the wolf out into the yard and threw him down into the deep well, never to be seen again.

Grandma thanked the woodcutter for saving them
and invited him for supper.
From that day on Little Red Riding Hood
promised she would never talk to strangers again.